Victoria Fredriksson

Bernie Bikes to the Indian Ocean

Bumblebee Books
London

BUMBLEBEE PAPERBACK EDITION

A CIP catalogue record for this title is
available from the British Library.

ISBN: 978-1-83934-460-2

Bumblebee Books is an imprint of
Olympia Publishers.

First Published in 2022

Bumblebee Books
Tallis House
2 Tallis Street
London
EC4Y 0AB

Printed in Great Britain

www.olympiapublishers.com

Dedication

I dedicate this book to my grandmother, May-Britt.

Further away than your fantasy can take you, but still closer than you think, there is a place you can't find on any map, one of the few places in northern Europe still unexplored by man. Somewhere in this wilderness there is a lake, and in the middle of the lake an island rests peacefully. This island is called Featherbay, and that has been its name since the first birds settled on the deserted island. The birds decided that Featherbay would be a sanctuary for all the birds in northern Europe. For the pigeons that stressed people kick at in the big cities, for cagebirds that managed to escape, and for the seagulls that have seen their beloved archipelago islands taken over by summer-celebrating humans. In Featherbay, all birds can live in peace and harmony with the knowledge that humans will never be able to find their hidden paradise. The largest group of birds living in Featherbay are migrating birds. They call Featherbay their home during the summer and fly to the Indian Ocean for the winter.

Another fall had arrived in Featherbay, and the migrating birds were in full preparation for their long journey to the Indian Ocean. Young migrating birds need to practice a lot before embarking on the journey for the first time. The hardest part when learning to fly is how to land, so a runway had been built for them to practice on. It was located right by the shore on the north side of Featherbay. On a crisp October morning, three young migrating birds were out on the runway. Their names were Bernie, Beaky and Wingy. Bernie had the strongest wings in his class and had already been given his flying certificate, so this morning he was out on the runway to help his two best friends; Beaky, who was shy and afraid of heights, and Wingy, who was heavily built, and had difficulties with stopping and putting his brakes on in time.

The three friends had just made it back from their first flight practice of the day, but Wingy, as usual, had problems with his brakes and ended up in the tall grass by the water.

"We need a longer runway," muttered Wingy, while he was shaking the water off his feathers.

"I don't think the runway is the problem," Bernie said with a laugh while he and Beaky sat down next to the runway to rest for a bit.

Wingy soon joined them, Bernie took out a thermos from his backpack, and the three friends enjoyed some hot chocolate Bernie's mum had made them.

"Bernie, do you ever think I'll be able to land properly?" asked Wingy nervously. "I'm getting sick and tired of always ending up in the water."

"I'm sure you will," Bernie said, encouraging. "You are getting better and better with each day that passes."

"I'm still terribly afraid of heights," complained Beaky while sipping the hot chocolate. "A bird afraid of heights, sounds like a joke."

"I'm sure everything will work out," Bernie said calmly, "with a little more practice it's not going to feel so scary. The three of us will all make it to the Indian Ocean, that is what we migrating birds are made for.

"And it's getting close to departure," Wingy said with a shiver. "Every morning is a bit chillier than the last."

The three friends' break was interrupted by a weird sound coming from the bushes on the other side of the runway.

"Is there a rooster in the bushes?" Wingy asked, confused. "I hear 'cock-a-doodle-do', but maybe I hit my head too many times on the runway."

"It does sound like a rooster," Bernie said, "but what is a rooster doing in the bushes?"

"Maybe it's the Seagulls pulling another one of their famous pranks?" Beaky said.

"Perhaps," Bernie said, "but I think we should investigate."

The three friends went closer to the weird bush making the 'cock-a-doodle-do' sound and looked curiously at what they could see behind the leaf and branches.

What they saw was the Rooster Bob, sitting collapsed with tears running down his feathers.

"What are you doing here Bob?" Bernie asked, surprised. "Shouldn't you be in the hen house?"

When Rooster Bob saw the three birds looking at him, he tried to dry his tears, but immediately started crying again.

"Come out of the bush and sit down with us," Bernie said. "You can get some hot chocolate and tell us what's wrong."

They all sat down by the runway and Bob tried to talk. It was not easy for the three friends to understand what Bob was saying, as he was either crying or going 'cock-a-doodle-do', but sometimes a few words came out of him.

"It's Franny," Bob finally said. "She does not want to marry me."

The hen Franny was Bob's girlfriend. They had been together longer then the three friends could remember.

"What are you saying?" said Beaky. "The two of you are made for each other."

“I thought so too,” Bob said with his head hanging in despair.

“Did Franny give any explanation as to why she didn’t want to marry you?” Bernie asked.

“She says my ‘cock-a-doodle-do’ is off-pitch. She says it gives her a headache. I don’t think she wants to marry a rooster.”

“Did she say she did not want to marry a rooster?” Wingy asked.

“No,” Bob answered, "but what could else be the problem?”

“We’ll go to Featherbay’s birdsong therapist,” Bernie said, supporting. “I’m sure that will help.”

Bob once again burst into tears and started crowing ‘cock-a-doodle-do’. He was so off pitch the three friends had to put their wings over their ears, but suddenly Bob stopped crying and lifted his head up.

“Now I know!” Bob said excitedly. “My ‘cock-a-doodle-do’ may be off-pitch, but if I show Franny I have other talents maybe she will change her mind!”

“What talents do you have?” Wingy asked, trying not to sound condescending.

“Well, let me think,” Bob said, and was quiet for a bit before shouting, “I can fly!”

The three friends looked at each other in confusion before Bernie said, “But Bob, you are a rooster, and roosters can hardly fly a meter.”

“Has Bob lost his mind?” Wingy whispered into Beaky’s ear. “I can’t be the only one hitting my head quite often.”

Bob looked at the three friends with a pleading look before saying, "But if I could borrow a pair of wings I could fly."

"You want to borrow our wings?!" Wingy said in shock.

"Oh please," Bob said, "just for a little bit, I just want to fly to the hen house, and when Franny sees me flying, she will be so impressed she will want to marry me immediately!"

"But our wings are the most important thing we have," Wingy said while he corrected his wings. "We can't just let other birds that can't fly borrow them."

"I will only borrow them for a short little while," Bob insisted. "You won't even have the time to miss them."

"Well, you can't borrow my wings," Wingy said, "There is a problem with the breaks, and a bird without flying habit is going to crash land."

"You can't borrow mine either," Beaky said, "They are not strong enough yet, so it is difficult to steer. The only one of us that has a flying certificate is Bernie."

Bernie sat quiet and thought about it for a while. He really wanted to help his friend, but to let someone borrow a bird's most important possession was a big decision. But when he saw how distraught Bob the Rooster was, he made his mind up.

"Okay, Bob, you may borrow my wings."

Bob once again started with his 'cock-a-doodle-do'. This time out of joy, but still very much off-pitch.

"Thank you thank you," Bob repeated, "Franny will be so impressed that I'm a flying rooster."

"Just remember that this is a loan," Bernie said with a determined voice. "Just to the hen house and then straight back to the runway."

"Certainly," Bob said and nodded his head, making his comb go back and forth.

"Bernie," Wingy said and pulled him to the side. "Are you really sure about this?"

"Yes," Bernie answered, "Bob is my friend and I want to help him."

Bernie began to gently remove his wings and attach them to Bob.

"Take good care of my wings now Bob," Bernie said, "Follow me and I will show you how to use them."

Bernie gave Bob a crash course in the art of flying. Bob learned how to flap the wings and how to take off and land.

"Okay Bob, do you feel ready to fly?" Bernie asked.

"I'm ready," Bob said, flapping the wings with confidence.

"Just to the hen house and then straight back here, right?" Wingy said while crossing his wings in front of him, trying to look scary.

"Yes, yes," Bob said impatiently and got ready for take-off.

"Good luck Bob!" Bernie shouted while Bob took off from the runway.

"This is amazing!" an excited Bob called out. "Flying is amazing!"

Bob made a wide turn over the three friends and Wingy annoyingly said, "Straight for the hen house Bob!"

Bob then started flying towards the hen house located on the south side of Featherbay. After a while, the three friends were no longer able to see the flying rooster.

"It must be the most stupid thing I've seen in my whole life," muttered Wingy, "a rooster flying with borrowed wings. Well, I hope it impresses the hens."

"I really hope he will be back soon," Beaky said nervously. "If anyone finds out Bernie let a rooster borrow his wings, we are all going to be in a lot of trouble."

"Who will find out?" Bernie said. "Soon Bob will return with my wings, but it does feel very strange without them, like a piece of me is missing."

"Should we do some fishing while we wait for the flying idiot rooster?" suggested Wingy. "After all, we must eat plenty in preparation for our long journey to the Indian Ocean."

The three friends starting swimming around in the shallow water that surrounds Featherbay, trying to catch some fish. They laughed and had so much fun at Bernie's failed attempts to try to catch fish without his wings that they lost track of time.

"Where is Bob?" Beaky finally asked while he swallowed a perch.

"Didn't your parents teach you not to talk with fish in your mouth?" Wingy asked annoyed.

"At least I'm catching some fish," Beaky said proudly, "That is more than I can say about you, don't you agree Bernie?"

Bernie was not listening to his friends. He was looking at the sky, the sun had slowly started moving towards the horizon. Bernie realized that Bob had been gone for hours, considerably longer than it takes to fly to and back from the hen house.

"Maybe he had to stop on the way," Wingy said when he saw his friend staring at the horizon. "Maybe a problem occurred with the wings."

"Not with Bernie's wings," Beaky said, "they are the best and strongest in our entire class."

"The two of us will fly and look for the flying rooster," Wingy said to Beaky.

"Okay," said Bernie, trying to hide the panic in his voice, "but you are probably right, he had to stop along the way."

Wingy and Beaky immediately got on the runway and got ready for take-off.

"We will find Bob," Wingy said to Bernie. "He is probably in a tree going 'cock-a-doodle-do'."

The two friends flew away in the direction of the hen house to search for Bob and Bernie's wings. Left alone on the runway was Bernie trying to hold back his tears. Bernie looked out over the water that soon would freeze to ice, by which point he and the rest of the migrating birds should have arrived at the Indian Ocean. Bernie shook his head trying to push away the negative thoughts. *Of course Bob would return with his wings*, Bernie told himself. *It was a loan, and if you borrow something you must return it.*

After what felt like an eternity Bernie could see his two friends approaching the runway, but Bernie could not see a trace of either Bob or his wings. Beaky and Wingy touched down on the runway, and for the first time Wingy made a perfect landing, then rushed over to Bernie.

"I am so sorry Bernie," Wingy said, trying to catch his breath, "but we can't find Bob or your wings."

"Did you fly to the hen house to ask Franny?" Bernie wondered, terrified.

"Yes," Beaky said, who now also ran up to Bernie. "Franny said that Bob did make it to the hen house, but Franny had been so upset at the sight of Bob as a flying rooster she told him that she wants to marry a rooster proud of being a rooster, not a rooster pretending to be a migrating bird."

"And that a rooster with borrowed wings don't belong in a hen house," Wingy added, "Bob had not said a single word, not even a 'cock-a-doodle-do'. He just flew away. Franny has no idea where he could have flown to."

Bernie fell to the ground in despair.

"I'm sure Bob will return," Beaky said, "he probably got so excited about having wings he wanted to fly some more."

The three friends sat down on the runway waiting to see a rooster with borrowed wings appear, but as time went on and still no sight of Bob, Bernie had to realize his wings had been stolen, and that he now was a migrating bird without wings.

"These roosters are unreliable," Wingy said, shaking his head in disappointment.

"But I didn't think he was capable of stealing," Beaky said, shivering as a cool breeze came across the runway.

Then the three friends heard a deep, dull voice coming from the water.

"Why are you three being lazy birds sitting on the runway? You are supposed to be practicing for your departure to the Indian Ocean."

The three friends turned to the water where they could see that the deep, dull voice talking to them belonged to Flock-

Leader Richard, who was out on his late night swim around Featherbay. Flock-Leader Richard was a stately swan; he was a firm but fair flock-leader and was very well liked by the residents of Featherbay. The three friends immediately got up from the runway, allowing Flock-Leader Richard to notice that Bernie was missing his wings.

"Young bird," Richard said with a harsh voice while extending his long swan neck. "Where are your wings?"

"I let someone borrow them," Bernie said silently.

"What are you saying?" Richard said, upset. "A migrating bird should never take off their wings, that is the most important rule for a migrating bird. Who did you let borrow your wings?"

"The rooster, Bob," Bernie said, embarrassed, his eyes fixed on the ground unable to look at Richard. "But he has not returned them. Wingy and Beaky have looked for him, but both Bob and my wings are gone with the wind."

"Young man," Richard said, "that is the reason we have the rule that you must never take off your wings. Unfortunately, not everyone understands the meaning of a loan, that you must return what you have borrowed."

Richard looked at Wingy and Beaky.

"Have you searched the entire Featherbay?"

"Yes," Wingy answered factually, "Rooster Bob flew to the hen house, after that he seems to have flown away. We have searched all over Featherbay, but I am sorry to come to the conclusion that Bob must have left Featherbay and have done so with Bernie's wings."

Flock-Leader Richard remained quiet for a bit before

looking at Bernie with disappointment.

"This simply could not happen. You are a migrating bird and the winter is approaching, you must go to the Indian Ocean."

"I'm sorry," Bernie said, still looking at the ground. "I was only trying to help a friend."

"I shall now return to my late-night swim," Flock-Leader Richard said, "It's during my late-night swims that I figure out solutions to all problems the residents of Featherbay need my help with. The three of you will wait here while I do so!"

The three friends did not move a muscle while Richard swam in circles in the shallow waters, deeply immersed in his own thoughts. After a while Richard began swimming towards the three friends. Had the smart swan managed to find a solution?

"Young birds, I have now solved the problem of Bernie's stolen wings," Richard declared.

"Yes, Flock-Leader Richard," Bernie said expectantly, "what is your solution?"

"Bruno the Bear," Richard said.

The three birds looked at each other in confusion. Bruno the Bear was the only resident in Featherbay that was not a bird. He usually kept to himself in his nest on the eastern side of Featherbay.

"Excuse me Mr. Flock-Leader," Wingy said gently, "but how can Bruno the Bear be the solution to Bernie's stolen wings?"

"That I will now tell you," Richard said proudly, "As all of you already know it has always been a mystery how Bruno the Bear made it to Featherbay. The most logical explanation would be that he swam here, but since he is paralyzed in his left front paw there must be another explanation. But he did manage to come to Featherbay, so at dawn you three young birds will go over to Bruno's nest and ask him to tell you how he got here. If we are in luck, the same way he came to Featherbay, the same way Bernie can make it to the Indian Ocean."

"But," said Bernie, "why would Bruno the Bear want to help us? Everyone knows he does not want anything to do with us birds, he just wants to be left alone."

"Tell Bruno this is an order from me," Richard said decidedly, "After all, I am the flock-leader of Featherbay, and I can make his stay here very difficult. I don't think he wants a gang of Seagulls pooping on his nest, for example."

"But…" Bernie said.

"No buts or excuses," Flock-Leader Richard said, determined, "You three young birds will at dawn make your way to Bruno's nest."

"Yes, Mr. Flock-Leader Richard," said the three friends unanimously.

"Well then," Richard said, "I hope the three of you have learned a lesson today. Now, get back to your bird's nest and rest for tomorrow."

Richard swam away and the three friends started to walk back to their bird's nest.

"How are we supposed to be able to knock on Bruno the Bear's door tomorrow?" Beaky said nervously, "No bird in Featherbay has ever dared to contact him."

"We just have to get brave," Wingy said, and pushed his chest forward in an attempt to look bigger. "This might be Bernie's only chance to make it to the Indian Ocean."

"I will walk to Bruno the Bear's nest alone tomorrow," Bernie said.

"Did you lose your mind together with your wings?" Wingy said, shocked.

"I'm the one that let Bob borrow my wings," Bernie said, "It's my fault, possibly putting the two of you in danger would not be right."

"We are your friends, and there is no way we are going to let you go to Bruno's nest by yourself," Beaky said.

"We will be there for you," Wingy added, "just like you always are there for us."

"Thank you," Bernie said, relieved, "thank you for being my friends, but how am I going to tell this to my parents? They will get so angry with me. My dad has always told me I must never take off my wings."

"Are your parents still awake?" Beaky asked surprised. "The sun has gone down."

"That is true," Bernie said, "I hope they are both asleep. Then I can wait to tell them about my stolen wings until we are back from Bruno's, and maybe I will have some good news then."

"If we make it back," muttered Beaky, but then Wingy punched him over the head with one of his wings.

"Ouch!" Beaky shouted.

"Hush now," Wingy whispered to Beaky, "don't scare Bernie."

"Did you hurt yourself?" Bernie asked Beaky, surprised.

"I just stepped on a rock," Beaky said, and jumped a little on one leg while Wingy was rolling his eyes at him.

The three friends had now arrived at Wingy and Beaky bird's nests; they lived next to each other in a large oak tree. Bernie's bird's nest was close by, high up in a pine tree.

"See you guys at dawn," Bernie said to his friends.

"Yes," said Wingy, "we will meet below your bird's nest."

Bernie stood and looked at his friends as they flew up to their bird's nests, and then he walked home alone to the big pine tree. His bird's nest was built at the top of the pine tree, but Bernie's dad had built a ladder for him so he could get up and down before he had learnt how to fly. Thankfully Bernie's dad had not removed the ladder. Bernie was as quiet as he possibly could be going up the ladder, and gently opened the door to the bird's nest. He drew a sigh of relief when he realized his parents had gone to bed. At the kitchen table was a bowl of fish soup, and next to it a note from Bernie's mom saying, "Don't forget to eat your dinner. You need a lot of energy for the long journey to the Indian Ocean".

While Bernie was eating his dinner, he thought about how his parents would react to the news that his wings were stolen, but Bernie could not think about that any more tonight, and he went to his room to get some rest. In the morning, he and his two friends would be the first birds to ever knock on Bruno the Bear's nest.

Bernie was so exhausted that he hardly noticed his alarm clock go off at dawn, but he woke up quickly when he realized that Wingy and Beaky probably already were waiting for him.

Just as Bernie had predicted, his parents were still asleep. Bernie wrote a note and put in on the kitchen table, "Went early to the runway, must practice for the departure". Bernie felt bad that he was lying to his parents, but he was not ready to tell the truth yet. He gently closed the door to the bird's nest and starting climbing down the ladder.

"Sleepy head!" he heard a voice shouting. Bernie got so scared he almost lost his grip and fell down.

"Hush," Bernie whispered to his friends who were waiting for him. "Don't wake my parents."

"Yes," Beaky said to Wingy, slapping him with his wing. "Didn't I tell to not yell like you think you are a seagull or something?"

"Yeah yeah," Wingy muttered while Bernie made his way to his friends.

"How are you today?" Beaky askes Bernie, concerned.

"Do you feel like a weight has lifted from your shoulders?" Wingy asked while blinking at Bernie.

"Wingy!" Beaky said angry, "Didn't I tell you not to tell that joke?"

"It's okay," Bernie said, "I feel okay, but very different. But I'm trying to think positive. Somehow, I will get to the Indian Ocean."

"That's the spirit," Beaky said, encouraging. "Well we better get going, after all it's a long walk."

"You don't need to walk with me," Bernie said, "you can fly there and we can meet at Bruno's nest."

"No way," Wingy said, "of course we will all walk together. And I've heard that walking is good exercise, and some birds say I need to lose a little weight before our departure."

"A little?" Beaky laughed. "You had five perches with creme sauce for breakfast!"

The three friends started their long walk. They needed to cross the entirety of Featherbay to get to the big 'Forest of the mist' on the eastern side of Featherbay. Bruno's nest was located in the darkest part of the forest.

"I hope we don't run into any seagulls," Beaky said, "They love to gossip, and if they see Bernie without his wings, all of Featherbay will know before the day is over."

"You love to gossip Beaky," Wingy said, laughing, "does that make you a seagull?"

Wingy and Beaky kept on with their bickering during the entire walk. They tried to get Bernie in a good mood, but they were also trying to hide their nervousness about meeting Bruno the Bear.

It was almost lunchtime when the three friends stopped for a second, and in front of them were trees so tall that it looked like they almost touched the sky. The forest was so thick no sunlight could make it to the ground.

"Is it just me, or does the forest look a bit threatening?" Beaky said nervously.

"Coward!" Wingy said, with his voice shivering a bit, which he hoped his friends did not notice.

"I guess it's a reason they call it 'Forest of the mist'", Bernie said.

"I'm starting to get hungry," Wingy complained, "I doubt there is anything to eat in that dark forest."

"Stop thinking about food," Beaky said, "We can't be

such chickens, let's go straight to Bruno's nest and knock on his door."

"Look who got all brave suddenly," Wingy muttered while the friends continued their walk. It didn't take long until they were in the middle of the forest.

"Forest of the mist," Wingy said, turning his head back and forth. "More like the pitch-black forest. I can hardly see my wings."

"Your eyes will get used to the dark," Bernie explained, "but does anyone know where in this forest Bruno's nest is?"

Beaky's eyes had already gotten used to the dark, so he pointed his wing straight ahead.

"Looking at the sign, I have my guess," he said.

"Sign?" Wingy said, confused, trying to see what Beaky pointed at.

But, soon all of the tree friends could see the sign that said, *No creatures with feathers beyond this point, this is Bruno the Bear's territory.*

"Oh well," Wingy said nervously, "I guess we better turn around. Bruno the Bear does not want any company."

"Remember what Flock-Leader Richard told us," Bernie said, "it is him and no one else that is the leader of Featherbay, and he ordered us here. Let's go!"

Bernie kept walking in a quick pace, with his friends trying to keep up.

"Bruno will probably eat us," Wingy complained.

Wingy hardly had time to finish his sentence before the tree friends saw a little tree hut built right by the entrance to a cave. They walked up to the tree hut where they could see another sign, *Bruno the Bear's nest. Private property.*

"Are we really sure about this?" Wingy said, "Feels like knocking on his door is like signing our death sentence."

"Wingy," Beaky said, "I'm getting tired of you being such a coward. And if you want to talk about a death sentence, remember Bernie's wings have been stolen. That is a death sentence for a bird."

"You are right," Wingy said, embarrassed. "We are here to help Bernie. And that is why I will knock on this door now."

Wingy walked up and knocked hard on the door to the tree hut three times. When he did that, a loud roar was heard from inside the tree hut.

"Help!" Wingy said, frightened, and tried to hide behind Bernie and Beaky. That did, however, not work out so well for him since he was bigger and taller than his both friends.

The door to the tree hut flew up, and the three friends hardly dared to look up at Bruno the Bear who was so big the three friends could easily fit under one of his paws.

"What could possibly presume you feather creatures to bother me?" Bruno said in a rage. "I am preparing to go into hibernation for the winter. Have you feather creatures lost all your manners and knowledge of reading? Did you not see the sign?"

"We are here visiting you today by the order of Flock-Leader Richard," Bernie said, trying to hide the fear in his voice.

"Flock-Leader Richard?" Bruno said, surprised.

"Yes," Beaky said, "and he wanted us to tell you that if you will not see us today and listen to what we have to say, he will send a bunch of seagulls to poop on your nest."

"Oh," said Bruno the Bear, "well, no one in their right mind wants a visit from seagulls, so I might as well let you in."

The three friends followed Bruno into his nest, where no feather creature have ever been before.

"I'm sorry if it's a little messy in here," Bruno said while moving some blankets, "but I am in preparation for a long winter. Please sit down by the table."

Bruno pointed at a large wooden table in the middle of his nest.

The three friends sat down at the wooden stools placed around the large table, their beaks could hardly reach over the table edge. Bruno also sat down at the table, and when he sat down on the stool the walls in his nest vibrated.

"It's very cozy in here," Beaky said, trying to be polite.

"You can stop with the courtesies," rumbled Bruno, "tell me instead what I possibly could help some small feather creatures with."

Bernie slowly started to tell his story, but he was so nervous he hardly knew where to begin.

"Well, I let a rooster borrow my wings, and, well, now it looks like I won't get them back, and…"

"Excuse me feather creature," Bruno said, "are you saying a rooster stole your wings?"

"Yes," Bernie said gently.

Bruno the Bear started to laugh loudly, making the walls in his nest shake once again.

"That is the funniest thing I've heard in years," said Bruno. "Oh, sorry, feather creature, please continue with your story."

"Well, I am a migrating bird," Bernie continued, feeling a little better now that Bruno seemed to find his situation entertaining, "and migrating birds need to spend the winter in the Indian Ocean, but now I can no longer fly there. So, Flock-Leader Richard had an idea that I should talk to you, because you are a Bear, and somehow you made it to Featherbay, and brown Bears usually don't swim so far, especially if they are paralyzed in one of their paws."

Bernie did not dare to look at Bruno who sat quiet for a while, thinking.

"You do have a clever leader," Bruno said at last. "Well, I guess there is no real reason for me to keep how I made it to Featherbay a secret. Come with me, feather creatures!"

Bruno got up from his stool with the friends jumping down from their stools, following him. They went to a little shed in connection to Bruno's nest, and Bruno unlocked the padlock, pushed the door open and turned on the light.

"Here," Bruno said, "here you have the answer of how I got to Featherbay!"

The three friends looked around in the little shed. They saw three toolboxes, one saw and a yellow bicycle in the middle of the shed.

"But can't you see feather creatures," Bruno said gesticulated with his one front paw, "a bicycle!"

"Yes, we can see that," Bernie said carefully, "but I don't understand what a bicycle has to do with you getting to Featherbay. You can't ride a bicycle on the water."

"I guess at first sight it does not look like there is anything special with this bicycle," Bruno said, walking up to it, "but with this bicycle you can ride on water!"

"What?" the three friends said at the same time.

"Oh yes," Bruno explained, "see, my dad was an inventor and he made me this bicycle as a gift so I could see the world. I have been paralyzed in my left front paw since birth, but my dad did not want that to stop me. After riding with my bicycle on the seven seas of the world, I ended up in Featherbay, and I felt at home here immediately. It does not matter to me that I am the only bear here, and since I don't have any plans of leaving, you can borrow my bike."

The three friends looked at each other with a sense of hope. Could this really be the answer they were looking for?

"But," Bernie said, "I don't know how to ride a bike, at least that is what I think, I've never tried."

"No problem," Bruno said proudly, "this bike is equipped with training wheels, so it gives both support and extra speed. And as if that was not enough, there is a turbo engine mounted on the rear wheel. It even has a breakwater function if you need to ride through a big wave. Let's say a big wave is approaching, then you just turn on the turbo engine, activate the breakwater function and you will do great."

The three friends burst out in loud cheer and started dancing around in Bruno's shed. Finally, they knew how Bernie could get to the Indian Ocean without his wings!

"Take it easy now feather creatures," Bruno said when he saw Wingy almost knock down one of his toolboxes with his wild dance.

The three friends stopped their joy dancing and Bernie asked curiously:

"But, can you ride a bike as fast as you can fly?"

"Well, I don't fly," Bruno said with a laugh, "but I would assume flying is faster, so it would be best if you start your bike ride to the Indian Ocean tomorrow."

"Wow," Bernie said, trying to grasp the idea that he, a migrant bird, would go on such a long journey on a bicycle.

"This is what we will do," Bruno said, "I will make sure the bike is top notch until tomorrow morning. Then we can meet at the beach by the runway in the morning, and you can practice riding the bike until you feel ready for departure."

"Okay," Bernie said, "thank you so much for your help, Bruno the Bear. I have been so sad since my wings got stolen."

"Just remember," Bruno said, "this is a loan, I will expect to get the bike back in the same condition as when you borrowed it."

"Of course," Bernie said, "I would never steal something from someone like Bob the Rooster did to me."

"Alright then," Bruno said, "off you go now feather creatures so I can work on the bike."

"Absolutely," Bernie said, "and thank you again, Bruno."

"Let's not make a big fuss over this," Bruno said. "I was ordered to help you by Flock-Leader Richard. I don't want feather creatures stopping by at any given moment asking for help."

"Of course not," Bernie said, "this will be our secret."

The three friends left Bruno's shed, and once again started dancing with joy, they didn't even get scared being in the dark forest. Bernie felt so relieved he now knew how he would get to the Indian Ocean without his wings. The three friends walked back to their bird's nests and decided to meet early next morning on the runway where Bernie would learn how to ride a bike. Bernie took a deep breath after he had climbed up the ladder to his bird's nest. Now it was time for him to tell his parents that his wings had been stolen, and he would ride a bike to the Indian Ocean. Bernie gently opened the door and saw his parents sitting at the dinner table, eating their supper as they usually did at this time in the evening, but it was their dinner guest that surprised Bernie.

"Flock-Leader Richard?" Bernie said surprised, "I didn't know we were expecting company."

Flock-Leader Richard slowly put down his silverware and wiped his beak with a napkin before saying, "It was not only for the delicious fish balls I decided to make a visit this evening. I wanted to discuss the situation with your stolen wings. I was very surprised to learn that your parents had no knowledge about that."

"That is correct," Bernie said, ashamed, "I have not told them yet; I was about to do so now."

"How could you let someone borrow your wings?" Bernie's dad said, standing up so fast from his chair that his bowl of fish balls flipped over, and the fish balls started to roll all over the table. "It is the most important possession for a migrant bird!"

"I trusted Bob the Rooster," Bernie said, staring at the wooden floor. "I thought he would give them back."

Bernie's mother walked up to give him a comforting hug.

"Don't be too hard on Bernie now," she said, "he was only trying to help a friend. You know how kind our Bernie has always been, and that is a good quality to have."

"But then these things happen," muttered Bernie's dad while he sat down at the table again. "Oh, these roosters, lying, stealing, and going 'cock-a-doodle-do' is all they do."

"Bob the Rooster can't go 'cock-a-doodle-do'", Bernie said in an attempt to lighten the mood. "He is terribly off-pitch."

Bernie's dad was still upset, and looked angrily at Bernie, saying, "You know son, what makes me the most upset about this mess is the fact that you did not come to us straight away when this happened. You made the choice to hide this from your parents, did you not think we would notice that your wings are missing?"

"I was going to tell you," Bernie insisted. "I thought you would be less disappointed in me once I figured out how I would get to the Indian Ocean without my wings."

"On that note," Flock-Leader Richard said, "what is the result from your excursion to Bruno the Bear's nest?"

"I'm going to borrow his bike!" Bernie said proudly.

The bird's nest went completely quiet; they could even hear a pinecone falling from a tree branch outside.

"I've had enough!" Bernie's dad shouted. "Just because he is a young migrant bird, Bruno the Bear thinks he can fool him with this ludicrous claim, a bike?"

"Calm down," Flock-Leader Richard said, "Bernie, can you tell us exactly what Bruno the Bear said?"

"Bruno cycled to Featherbay," Bernie explained, "on a bike his father built for him. You can ride the bike on water, and it has a turbo engine and a breakwater function, it even has training wheels!"

"Have you seen this bike?" Bernie's mother asked.

"Oh yes," Bernie said, dreamy, "it was the most beautiful yellow bike I have ever seen."

"Have you seen a bike before?" Bernie's dad asked.

"No," Bernie replied.

"This might actually work," Flock-Leader Richard said. "If Bruno did ride a bike from the mainland to Featherbay, I see no reason why Bernie should not be able to ride with it to the Indian Ocean."

"Not just from the mainland to Featherbay," Bernie said, "he has been riding his bike on all seven oceans of the world."

"My Bernie can do anything he puts his mind to," Bernie's mom said, determined.

"Okay then," Bernie's father said, "even if this is the stupidest thing I have ever heard, Bernie must go to the Indian Ocean somehow, so I guess he will ride this bike."

"Bernie, has a date been set for departure with the bike?" Flock-Leader Richard asked.

"Yes," Bernie said, "tomorrow morning I will meet Bruno on the runway for a lesson on how to ride a bike, and after that I will depart Featherbay. You can't ride a bike as fast as you can fly you see."

"Oh wow," Bernie's mom said, "departure tomorrow. Then I must start making hot chocolate you can bring for your journey. I must find our largest thermos."

Bernie's mom rushed into the kitchen while Flock-Leader Richard stood up from the table.

"Alright then," he said, "time for me to leave and spread

the word about your departure. I am sure all the inhabitants of Featherbay wants to see this bike and wish you good luck on your voyage. Have a good night's rest."

Then, Flock-Leader Richard gracefully flew out from the bird's nest.

"Yes, you better get to bed Bernie," his dad said, "you have a very long bike ride ahead."

"I will, Dad," Bernie said, and walked to his room. "I am sorry to have disappointed you."

Bernie's dad was the last one still sitting at the dinner table and a smile started to spread over his face; he was thinking about how his son would be the first migrant bird to ride a bike to the Indian Ocean.

"I don't believe you can find a prouder father," he said quietly.

Bernie's steps were eager and in anticipation as he walked down to the runway the following morning. He stopped for a second when he got there and closed his eyes. *When I open my eyes, I will see the most beautiful bicycle in the whole world*, he thought to himself. But at the same time, he got scared, what if Bruno the Bear had fooled him, and you can't ride the bike on water? What if he just wanted to play a prank on some silly migrating birds? Bernie then opened his eyes and saw Wingy, but he then drew a sigh of relief when Wingy took a step to the left, and he could then see the bike. The first rays from the morning sun were dancing over the bike making it almost glow.

"Wow," Bernie admired.

"There you are," Beaky said, who was holding on to the

bicycle's handlebars. "Come here, me and Wingy can't stop admiring the bicycle."

"Have you been here long?" Bernie asked.

"Your friends just arrived," Bruno said while he was pumping air into the wheels. "I have been here for hours rearranging the bicycle saddle and cleaning the turbo engine. Now the bike is ready for the long bike ride."

"Thank you so much, Bruno," Bernie said.

"My pleasure," Bruno said, "it actually feels really good being able to help someone. Mostly I'm just by myself in the Forrest of the Mist."

"Well, you avoid us feather creatures," Wingy said with a laugh.

"Yeah, yeah," Bruno said, a little embarrassed while he fumbled with a cloth filled with oil stains. "You three feather creatures are not so bad, but don't tell anyone I said that."

The three friends looked at each other with a smile. They suspected Bruno liked their company more than he would like to admit.

"Alright, time for you to get up on the saddle, Bernie," Bruno said, "time to learn how to ride a bike!"

"But what if I can't learn how to ride a bike?" Bernie said nervously.

"You will learn," Bruno said calmly, "and you have the training wheels on until you learn."

It was not so easy for a bird without wings to get up on the saddle, but Bernie figured it out after a little while. Bruno taught Bernie how to steer, how the breaks worked and how to activate the turbo engine and breakwater function. Bruno explained that you should not use the turbo engine and the breakwater function unless you really need to. That's because they crave a lot of power and they run on solar energy so it takes time for them to recharge. It was still very unsteady for Bernie to ride the bike without the training wheels, so Bruno decided to keep them on for him.

"That looks great!" Bruno said proudly after Bernie went back and forth on the runway on the bike. "Now it's time for you to ride on the water."

"Really?" Bernie said. "Am I really ready for that?"

Bruno lifted the bike into the shallow water with Bernie still sitting in the saddle holding on for dear life, with his beak on the handlebars for balance.

"We will never know until we try," Bruno said.

"Are you as nervous as me?" Beaky said to Wingy as they stood on the runway.

"It's hard for me to even believe my own eyes," Wingy said, "a bear helping a bird without wings to ride a bike on the water."

"You got that right," a voice behind them said. "If it wasn't Flock-Leader Richard who told me, I would never have believed it."

Wingy and Beaky turned around and saw Andy, one of the other migrating birds in their class. He curiously looked at the events unfolding in the shallow water, and was joined by his three older brothers. Behind them was an entire crowd of migrating birds, seagulls, swallows and pigeons.

"Is the entirety of Featherbay here?" Beaky said surprised.

"Do you think anyone would want to miss this?" Andy

said laughing. "This beats the Fish Pond during the Summer festival."

At the same moment, Bernie started to pedal in the water and, slowly but surely, the bicycle started to move across the water. It was a little unsteady, but he managed to go around in small circles in the shallow water.

"Hurray!" Bernie heard an unfamiliar voice shout and it was followed by load applauses and happy cheers.

Bernie took his eyes away from the bicycle handles and was able to see all of Featherbay gathered on the runway to cheer him on. Bernie lost his focus for a second, lost his balance and fell into the water. Bruno helped him up and said,

"Looks like we have an audience. None of us are used to this many feather creatures at once."

"I was not prepared to practice in front of this many birds," Bernie said shyly.

"You don't need any more practice," Bruno said proudly, "Now you can ride this bike and you are ready for departure."

"Wow!" Bernie said in disbelief, and started leading his bike up to the beach with his beak with Bruno next to him.

They had just made it up to the runway when Flock-Leader Richard landed just in front of them. He walked up to Bruno and reached out his wing that Bruno took in his paw.

"On the behalf of Featherbay I would like to thank you Bruno the Bear. You have shown great generosity and strength helping one of the inhabitants of Featherbay in one of his most trying times. I would hereby like to make you an honorary citizen of Featherbay."

Load applause broke out from all the gathered birds,

clapping their wings. Bruno first looked a little surprised, but he then went on to give Flock-Leader Richard a big hug that lifted him from the ground.

"Oh, thank you," Bruno said. "Featherbay really is the best place in the whole world!"

"You are welcome," Flock-Leader Richard said, "but can you be so kind and put me down now?"

Bruno put him down and Flock-Leader Richard quickly corrected his feathers before turning to Bernie and saying,

"We have no time to waste young bird. Immediately after you have said goodbye to your family and friends, it is time for you to depart for the Indian Ocean."

"Yes, Flock-Leader Richard," Bernie said, and gave the bike to Bruno.

First, Bernie walked up to his parents.

"Oh Bernie," his mom said, "you looked incredible on the bike. I have made some hot chocolate for you; I hope it will last for your entire journey."

Bernie's mom pulled out the biggest thermos Bernie had ever seen.

"Young man," Bernie's dad said, "I brought along a fishing rod for you on your travel, so you will be able to fish."

"Thank you, Dad," Bernie said, "but will I really be able to find the way to the Indian Ocean?"

Bernie's dad leaned forward and put his hand on Bernie's chest.

"Yes, Bernie, you will, because what you have here is something all migrating birds have, and that makes us always able to find our way."

"What is that?" Bernie asked, confused.

"Your inner compass, my son. You will always find your way in life if you listen to it."

Then Bernie heard a 'cock-a-doodle-do', and saw Bob the Rooster's girlfriend, Franny, who made the way up to Bernie through the crowd.

"Oh, Bernie can you ever forgive me? I had no idea that Bob would steal your wings. Everything just went so wrong, I told Bob I can't marry him with his 'cock-a-doodle-do' being so off-pitch, I get a terrible headache. I told him there is help he can get for that, but instead he came flying with your wings. Then I told him I want to marry a rooster, not a migrating bird, but then he just flew away."

"It's not your fault, Franny," Bernie said, "and I was able to borrow a bike, so it will be okay."

Wingy and Beaky walked up to Bernie and they both gave him a hug.

"We will meet again in the Indian Ocean," Beaky said.

"Good luck Bernie," Wingy said, trying to hide a tear that went down his feathers.

"You are such a drama queen," Beaky said, and slapped him with his wing.

"Are you ready now Bernie?" Flock-Leader Richard said.

All the eyes and feathers of Featherbay looked at Bernie as he shyly said,

"Yes, I am ready for my bike ride."

Loud applauses once again broke out in the audience while Bernie took the bag containing his fishing rod and thermos in his beak, and walked up to the bicycle.

Flock-Leader Richard stood next to Bernie saying, "If Bob the Rooster makes it back here, I will have a long talk with him. He needs to learn the meaning of a loan."

"Here is the bike, Bernie," Bruno said and handled him the yellow bike.

"Thank you," Bernie said, and put the bag with the thermos and fishing rod in the basket in the front. "I promise I will return the bicycle to you."

"I trust you," Bruno said, "but let's not forget the most important thing."

Bruno dug a bit in one of his toolboxes before he produced a weird-looking construction that he put on Bernie's head. The inhabitants of Featherbay looked curiously at the weird thing sitting on Bernie's head.

"A helmet," Bruno explained, "so your head doesn't get hurt if you fall."

Once again applauses could be heard all over.

"Oh, yes," Flock-Leader Richard said, "that truly is a fabulous invention. Perhaps Bruno would consider making some of these head protecting devices for our young birds learning to fly. Some of them are very clumsy and fly into trees quite frequently."

"I would love to," Bruno responded, "I love building things."

Bernie turned to the inhabitants of Featherbay and said, "Thank you for all your support, I will represent Featherbay well out on the ocean. And to all you migrating birds, I will see you again in the Indian Ocean!"

"Go Bernie!" Wingy and Beaky shouted as Bernie took

his first pedal stroke on the water.

To the sound of the birds of Featherbay cheering him on, Bernie started his journey. From time to time, he turned his head around to see the crowd of birds waving at him with their wings, but once he had turned left to get out of the bay, he could no longer see his family and friends. This truly was not how he thought he would make his first trip to the Indian Ocean, but Bernie was excited to start his great adventure.

During the first phase of the bike ride it was not hard for Bernie to find the way; the seagulls showed the way since they were on their way to catch some fish in deeper waters.

But the further away from Featherbay Bernie got, the more distant the cries of the seagulls got until everything around him got quiet. Bernie stopped pedaling and looked around. All he could see in every direction was water. Bernie squeezed his eyes, focusing on the horizon with the hope of seeing mainland somewhere, but it was just water everywhere. Then Bernie remembered what his dad said. His inner compass. *It must be now I need to use my inner compass.* He closed his eyes and did not think of anything particularly, waiting for his inner compass to show itself, but he could not feel a thing besides the bike slowly rocking in the same pace as the small waves.

Maybe I don't have an inner compass? Bernie thought and opened his eyes in despair. *How am I going to get to the Indian Ocean without it? I might end up in Antarctica, oh wouldn't that be typical, a migrating bird not able to find the Indian Ocean.* Bernie shook his head in disappointment and slowly started to pedal again to make his way back to Featherbay. If he did not have an inner compass, it would be better to go back and ask one of the older migrating birds to draw him a map to the Indian Ocean, but Bernie then realized to his horror he did not know the way back to Featherbay. He was lost.

"Oh no," Bernie said loudly. "Not only don't I have any wings, I don't have any sense of direction either."

Bernie collapsed over the bicycle handlebars. But in the middle of his despair, he suddenly felt a warm sensation, it felt like it came from inside his chest and spread all over his body. Suddenly he could see a map of the whole world in front of him, and the way to the Indian Ocean was as crystal-clear as the chilly autumn air.

"Oh, silly me," Bernie told himself, laughing. "A bird with no sense of direction, how could that be? Finding the Indian Ocean is going to be a piece of cake."

With his newly discovered confidence, Bernie started riding the bicycle. He told himself riding the bicycle would be the only thing he would do, and only take breaks when he got hungry or needed to sleep. *Indian Ocean, here I come!*

The first three days on the ocean were mostly uneventful. There was only a slight breeze, almost no waves and the sun was shining with the exception for a cloud once in a while that blocked the sun. Bernie could feel how the chilly autumn air had been replaced by a warm breeze, so he knew his inner compass was guiding him the right way. Whenever he got hungry, he took a break from riding the bike and took out his fishing rod. However, Bernie did not have much success with the fishing and so far, he had only made one catch, one little mackerel, but Bernie would not give up so once again, he took out his fishing rod to see if his luck might change this day, and his tummy had started to rumble from hunger. He dangled his fishing rod while his mind went a million miles away. He wondered about his friends Wingy and Beaky; had they been able to get their flight certificate for departure to the Indian Ocean yet? Bernie could not help but to smile when he thought about Wingy ending up in the tall grass by the water instead of managing to stop on the runway. Bernie really did miss his family and friends, and that he was not able to make his first trip to the Indian Ocean together with them. But when he sat there in the middle of the ocean with his fishing rod, he still felt grateful to be a part of this adventure, even if hunger was a constant reminder.

"Hello there, sailor!"

Bernie got so scared by the bright voice that he almost lost his fishing rod. He was also shocked to see who the bright voice belonged to. It was the most beautiful bird he had ever seen, and that bird was now sitting on his bicycle handlebars.

"Hi," the bird said, "my name is Can-Can and I'm a Canary bird, what is your name?"

Can-Can's feathers were in all colors of the rainbow, and she had big turquoise eyes that made Bernie think about what his parents had told him about the turquoise water in the Indian Ocean. Can-Can's beautiful eyes were covered with the longest eyelashes Bernie ever seen.

"Are you okay?" Can-Can said, concerned. "You don't say anything, maybe I am bothering you, should I fly away?"

Bernie had gone completely speechless by the beauty of Can-Can, but he definitely did not want Can-Can to fly away, so he managed to say a few words.

"Hi…hi, I'm Bernie. I'm a migrating bird."

"Well, I didn't mean to scare you so you almost lost your fishing rod," Can-Can continued, "but I have never seen a bird ride a bicycle before, I was very curious."

"That is okay," Bernie said, "and, well, I have not had much luck fishing lately."

"Why don't you have any wings?" Can-Can wondered curiously.

"I let a rooster borrow them," Bernie explained, "but he never gave them back, so now I'm riding a bike to the Indian Ocean instead."

"Great, then, that you are so good at riding a bike," Can-Can said while her long eyelashes started to flutter as a warm breeze came across them.

"I have training wheels on the bike," Bernie explained, "it makes riding a bike easy."

"But why do you have to ride the bike all the way to the Indian Ocean?" Can-Can asked. "Can't you just spend the winter here?"

"Where am I?" Bernie asked.

"The Canary Islands!" Can-Can said, and spread her wings. "Don't you listen to anything I say, I'm a Canary bird!"

"There are no Canary birds where I come from," Bernie said.

"Of course, not silly, we only live on the Canary Islands. So why not spend the winter here instead?"

"I can't, even if it is very tempting," Bernie said, "I must ride this bike to the Indian Ocean, my family and friends will be expecting me to arrive."

"That is a shame," Can-Can said, disappointed, "but tell me, what is that weird construction on your head?"

"It's a bicycle helmet," Bernie explained, "It's to protect my head.

"You look good in it," Can-Can said.

"Thank you," Bernie said while looking into Can-Can's big eyes.

Then Bernie heard splashing and someone shouting,

"Help me! Please, help me!"

Bernie desperately tried to locate who was calling for help, when suddenly a dolphin cracked the water surface right by the bicycle.

"Help me! Help me!" the dolphin kept repeating.

"What do you need help with?" Bernie asked.

"Look over there," Can-Can said, pointing with her wing, "I think I know what's going on."

Bernie looked at the direction Can-Can was pointing and saw a giant creature floating on the water. The only creature Bernie had ever heard of being that size was a whale.

"Is it a whale?" Bernie asked.

Can-Can rolled her big, beautiful eyes before saying,

"I can tell you are not from here. That is a ship, full of human beings. I suspect it's a dolphin catcher ship, they come to this area sometimes to catch dolphins so the humans can look at them in captivity."

"That is right," said the dolphin in horror, and then Bernie could see a small dolphin baby next to the larger dolphin. "They try to catch me and my baby, I can easily swim fast enough to hide from them, but my baby can't swim that fast yet. Please help me!"

"How can I help?" Bernie asked.

"Can you take my baby and ride the bike as fast as you can to the closest island?" the dolphin said. "I will come for her as soon as it safe."

Then, Bernie remembered his turbo engine.

"Yes, I do have a turbo engine. Can-Can, are we close to an island?"

"There is one very close by," Can-Can answered.

"Please hurry," the dolphin mother said, while placing her baby in the basket in the front of the bicycle. "I will come for her, but I must leave now before the humans find me."

The dolphin disappeared under the water surface before Bernie and Can-Can could even notice.

"Fast, Bernie!" Can-Can shouted, "The island is just ahead."

"Yes, Can-Can, as soon as I find the button to the turbo engine."

Bernie found the button and pressed it with his beak, and with an earsplitting roar the bicycle went into top speed.

"Oh wow," Can-Can said, trying to hold on to the bicycle handlebars while consoling the crying dolphin baby.

It did not take long for an island to appear in front of them.

"The breaks, the breaks!" Can-Can shouted. "Or we will crash!"

Bernie turned off the turbo engine and pulled the brakes with all the power he had left in his legs, and at the last minute the bicycle was able to stop in the water just by a deserted beach.

"That was a close call," Bernie said.

Bernie looked around. The beach had a couple of palm trees slowly moving in the warm breeze, but it looked like they were all alone on the beach.

"Does no one else live on this island?" Bernie asked Can-Can.

"Nobody does on this part of the island," Can-Can replied.

"What are we going to do with the dolphin baby?" Bernie asked.

"She must be in the water," Can-Can replied, "I will lift her down from the bike."

Can-Can gently put the dolphin baby down in the shallow water at the beach.

"When do you think her mother will return?" Bernie asked, worried.

"It won't be long," Can-Can replied, "let's sit down on the beach for now."

"These humans," Bernie said, "I have heard so much about them but never seen them in real life. My parents tell me they put birds in cages, but they do the same to dolphins too?"

"They put any animal they can in cages," Can-Can said. "Some animals don't mind, but the humans never ask permission first."

The two birds sat down on the beach, and after a while Can-Can asked, "Do you mind taking your helmet off?"

"Oh," Bernie said while removing his bicycle helmet. "I had forgotten I had it on me."

"Now I can see more of my hero," Can-Can said. "You

were so brave."

Bernie hoped that Can-Can could not see how he blushed behind his feathers. Can-Can slowly leaned over Bernie's shoulder and Bernie hardly dared to move a feather. Can-Can rested her head right where Bernie's wings used to be attached, and Bernie was ashamed thinking Can-Can would not think he was not a real bird without his wings. It was almost like Can-Can could read his mind when she said,

"It does not matter to me you don't have any wings, Bernie. To be a bird is about a lot more than just having wings, and you are the bravest bird I have ever met."

The birds sat on the beach with the wonderful palm trees covering them just looking out on the ocean, and Bernie had almost forgotten how they got there when they heard a voice coming from the water.

"My baby! My baby!"

The dolphin mother had made it back to the beach and the tiny dolphin baby threw himself into his mother's arms.

"You are my heroes," the dolphin mother announced, "I will be grateful for you until the end of times."

"It's Bernie you should thank," Can-Can said.

"Tell me," the dolphin mother said, "is there anything I can do to repay you for saving the life of my baby?"

"Oh no," Bernie said, "we were just happy to help."

"Actually, there is something you could do for him," Can-Can responded.

"Anything," the dolphin mother said.

"Well," Can-Can continued, "even if Bernie can ride a bike better than most birds can fly, he is not so good at catching fish."

"That can be arranged," the dolphin mother said, "me and my baby will be back soon."

The dolphin and her baby disappeared under the water's surface, and minutes later they were back with mouths full of fish.

"Where would you like us to put the catch of the day?" the dolphin mother asked.

Bernie led his bike to the water, and the dolphins put all the fish in the front basket of the bicycle.

"I will spread the word of your heroism among the rest of the dolphins," the dolphin mother said. "Every dolphin you will meet on your journey will bring you plenty of fish, you will never have to ride your bike hungry."

"Thank you so much," Bernie said.

"I am the one that should be thanking you," the dolphin mother said, "the dolphins of the sea will be forever grateful."

The dolphin mother and her baby started to swim away, and Bernie and Can-Can were once again alone at the beach.

"You are my hero!" Can-Can shouted, putting her wings around Bernie. "Are you sure you can't stay on the Canary Islands for the winter?"

"I must go," Bernie said quietly, "I am a migrating bird, and I must get to the Indian Ocean. I would have happily stayed with you here otherwise."

"I guess I just to have to keep an eye out for you then," Can-Can said, "at some point you must return on your bike."

"Yes of course," Bernie said, and lit up. "Will you really be watching for me?"

"Absolutely," Can-Can said, "I never miss a thing going on the route out here, a bird on a bicycle or a ship, I never miss a single thing."

"So, I will you see you again?" Bernie asked hopefully.

"If you want to," Can-Can answered, "then I can show you the Canary Islands."

"I would love that," Bernie responded.

Can-Can gave Bernie a kiss on the cheek and Bernie felt once more how he started to blush.

"It's time for me to head back to my bird's nest," Can-Can said, "until the next time my hero."

Bernie watched as Can-Can flew away, and after a while he could no longer see her rainbow-colored feathers.

"Wow," Bernie thought, "is this how falling in love feels? No, I have to get myself together, I have an Indian Ocean to get to."

Bernie once more started to ride the bicycle. He had only gone a short distance when he realized he had forgotten his helmet on the beach and had to go back to get it. *It's not good being this woozy when you ride a bike*, Bernie thought while he put on his helmet. He could then see how Can-Can had lost one of her rainbow-colored feathers on the beach. Bernie picked it up with his beak.

"I am going to save this forever," he said out loud, "and I am going to show it to Wingy and Beaky, otherwise they are never going to believe me when I tell them about Can-Can." Bernie put the feather on his fishing rod, then he got on his bike once again to continue his journey.

Once he had covered some distance, he saw a terrifying

sight close to the horizon. This time he knew what he saw, it was humans in their floating machines. It was not the same floating machine as before; this one was smaller. Bernie almost froze in horror. What if the humans would catch him, and he would spend the rest of his life as a bird in a cage? Then he would never get to see his family again. The floating machine started to get closer, and Bernie hoped the turbo engine had got enough power back so he could get out of there fast. Bernie pressed the button in a frenzy, but nothing happened. The turbo engine had not regained its power yet. Then Bernie started to pedal the bike as fast as he could, but when he started to hear shouts from the floating machine, he knew he had been discovered.

"Look over there!" he heard a voice saying. "A bird riding a bicycle, that is certainly something you don't see every day. Or maybe I have been in the sun for too long and started to hallucinate?"

Bernie turned his head back and saw a human looking at him from the deck of the floating machine.

"Do you really expect me to believe that you are looking at a bird riding a bike on the water?" Bernie heard another human voice saying. "I will not get up from this comfortable sun chair to look, and if you really believe that, I suggest that you go below deck and rest, because you must have had too much to drink."

"Suit yourself," said the other voice, "well, I'm going to take a picture so I can show you later what you missed."

Bernie was blinded by a sharp flashing light. He thought maybe that was a weapon by the humans to catch birds. Bernie kept on riding the bike as fast as he could, but after a while he was so out of breath, he had to take a break. He hardly had the guts to turn around and look, maybe the floating machine was right behind him. But when he had the courage to turn around, he could see that the floating machine was heading the other way towards the horizon.

Bernie took some deep breaths while the waves the floating machine had created made the bicycle go up and down in the water. *I guess the humans on the floating machine did not want a bird to put in a cage*, Bernie thought. Bernie decided it was time to rest. To get some new strength, he had some of the fish the dolphin mother brought him. He wondered how many more adventures he would be a part of on the ocean.

The following days on the ocean were peaceful. The sun was shining during the day, and during the night the moon would light up the dark ocean. Bernie really had the time to enjoy his bike ride on the calm ocean. Every dolphin he encountered gave him fish as the rumor had spread about his heroism saving the dolphin baby, just as the dolphin mother had promised him. The days and nights on the ocean had started to become routine. Bernie would only take a break from riding the bike if he needed to eat or sleep. He was careful not to sleep for too long, since it is important to pay attention so you don't get caught in any powerful currents that could lead you off course. It was another early morning, as some dolphins showed up next to Bernie and the bike.

"Hello, migrating bird," one of the dolphins said, "do you need any fish?"

Bernie glanced at the basket in the front of the bicycle that was overcrowded with fish, and answered,

"Thank you, dolphin, but I have more fish than I can eat."

"Okay," the dolphin replied, "really fine fish you got there, but when you are a hero that is what you deserve."

Bernie felt how he once again started to blush; he was not used to be called a hero.

"But then let me take the time to give you a warning," the dolphin continued.

"A warning?" Bernie said, worried.

"Have you heard of the shark passage?"

"Shark passage?" Bernie shouted, almost falling of the bike.

"Yes," the dolphin continued, "it's where the sharks gather to eat, but there are signs located when you are getting close to it. The signs will show the way to a detour around the shark passage. So just follow the signs and you will be fine."

"Okay," Bernie said and swallowed loudly, "that does sound creepy, I have never seen a shark and I don't wish to do so either."

"Don't worry friend," the dolphin said calmly, "there are plenty of signs, you will not be able to miss the detour. I would also like to inform you that a big storm is on the way, the storm will, however, go west, so you don't have to ride through it."

"Thank you," Bernie said, "it would have been a little exciting to go through a storm though, this bike is equipped with a turbo engine and breakwater function for encountering bad weather and storms."

"Trust me, bird," the dolphin said, "this storm is not anything you want to encounter, it is the biggest storm we have seen for years. But like I said, you are not on a collision course with it."

"Thank you so much for telling me about the shark passage and the storm," Bernie said, relieved.

"I wish you good luck on your journey," the dolphin said, before disappearing below the water surface.

Bernie was once again alone on his journey, and he decided to keep riding the bike for a while longer before it was time for dinner. Occasionally he looked up at the sky, wondering if the migrating birds had passed over him yet on the way to the Indian Ocean. Bernie missed flying, there was something special about being up in the sky, looking down at the world below. He also wondered where his wings were now, where could Bob possibly have gone with his wings? *Not very far though*, Bernie reasoned, *he was probably back in Featherbay getting a reprimand from Flock-Leader Richard.*

At sunset Bernie decided it was time for him to eat his dinner. He had some of the fish the dolphins had given him, and they tasted divine. They tasted so good; Bernie could not stop eating. Finally, he was so stuffed he could not have another bite. *I should continue to ride the bike*, Bernie thought, but his tummy was so full he could not pedal. *I should rest for a bit and digest this food*, Bernie decided, and leaned back. *Just for a little while and watch this beautiful sunset*. He pretended Can-Can was there watching the sunset with him, and before he knew it, he had fallen into a deep sleep.

Suddenly, Bernie woke up. For a moment he did not know where he was, and though he was back in his bird's nest in Featherbay. He then realized he was on a bike in the middle of the ocean, and the sun was shining bright. *Have I slept through the night?* he wondered. *I was just going to rest my eyes for a bit.*

"Oh no," Bernie said out loud, "if I slept for this long, I could have drifted off course."

Bernie stood up on the pedals, trying to get a better view, but, not surprisingly, all he could see was water. Bernie sat down again and tried to focus so he could feel his inner compass. His eyes got wide when he realized he had drifted off course, straight to the west. Bernie immediately started to pedal to turn the bike around. *I will never eat that many fish again*, he promised himself.

After riding the bike for a while, he calmed down, how bad could it be? At the most, he might arrive at the Indian Ocean one day later than planned, no big deal, but suddenly Bernie felt how the bike started to move very slowly, no matter how much he pedaled. Was there something wrong with the bike? Bernie looked down at the water and could see that he was surrounded by big brown ropes. He picked one up with his beak to investigate. Bernie had never seen anything like it but it was almost impossible to bike through the thick ropes. After trying for a while Bernie decided it was best to start the turbo engine to get some extra power. But at the same time, he was about to start the turbo engine, so many of the ropes had entangled in the wheels so the bike fell over and Bernie ended up in the water. Bernie managed, however, to turn the bike up right again, and Bernie got back on the saddle. But, then he could see that his fishing rod had loosened from the bike and was floating on some ropes nearby.

"Can-Can's feather!" Bernie shouted.

He was not about to let the only thing he had left from Can-Can disappear. Bernie tried once more to get the bike moving, but it was not going anywhere. So, he threw himself back in the water to get to the fishing rod. Bernie, however, had forgotten that to swim without his wings was pretty much impossible. Bernie grabbed ahold of some of the ropes with his beak and feet and was able to stay above the water surface.

"Oh no!" Bernie thought, "How could I be so stupid and jump off the bike?"

Bernie was fighting against his tears as his beak started to hurt from holding on to the ropes. Everything started to look hopeless when Bernie suddenly could feel land underneath his feet.

What is this? Bernie wondered, confused. *There is no land in sight?*

Whatever it was that he was resting his feet on was big and growing, and it was so big that the bike and the fishing rod with Can-Can's feather also rested on the solid surface. A roar could be heard at the same time as water came out from a hole on the land.

"I certainly hope you have a good explanation for this?" Bernie heard a deep and dark voice say.

"What?" Bernie said, and looked around. "Who is talking to me?"

An eye then opened below Bernie's feet; the eye was almost bigger than Bernie.

"Help!" was the only thing Bernie managed to say.

"There is no reason to be scared bird," he heard the voice

say, “I am a gentle giant, a blue whale to be exact. How did you heard about us?”

“I have heard about whales,” Bernie answered, “but I have never seen one. I did see a ship for the first time a few days ago, at first I thought that was a whale.”

The blue whale started laughing, and Bernie had to use all his balance to not slide down from the whale.

“You are entertaining,” the whale continued, “but I certainly do wonder why a bird is attempting to ride a bike through the Sargasso Sea? A more impossible task would be hard to find.”

“Sargasso Sea?” Bernie said, surprised. “I am on the way to the Indian Ocean, but I fell asleep and drifted off course. When I woke up, I was surrounded by these brown ropes.”

“These are no brown ropes,” the blue whale said, “it is Sargassum seaweed, you can find them everywhere in this sea, and that does make it a not very suitable place to ride a bike. That is why I was so surprised seeing you in distress, falling off the bike.”

“I was just about to turn on my turbo engine when I lost my fishing rod,” Bernie explained. “That’s why I jumped in the water.”

“You have fish for weeks in that basket on the bike,” the blue whale said, perplexed. “Why care so much about losing your fishing rod? No, wait, don’t answer,” the blue whale continued, “whales are very smart creatures. Could this have something to do with the rainbow-colored feather attached to the fishing rod?”

“Yes,” Bernie said, embarrassed.

"Oh, I see," the blue whale said, "well, I also remember the feeling of being young and in love, even though it was a very long time ago since I was young. However, you can't lose your mind over it, then you can get into a dangerous situation, like you did just now."

"I'm very sorry," Bernie said, "I'm so thankful you were here to save me."

"I'm always happy to help," the blue whale said. "Now go and get your bike and the fishing rod, just be careful and don't fall down in my blowhole."

Bernie gently walked on the whale and got the bike and the fishing rod.

"Good," the blue whale said, "now, hold on tight so you don't lose your balance, and I will swim out from the seaweed so you can ride the bike again."

The blue whale started to move slowly, and Bernie could hardly believe he was riding a whale.

"My friends in the Indian Ocean are not going to believe me when I tell them I got a ride from a whale," Bernie said, excited.

"It is to the Indian Ocean you are heading?" the blue whale said.

"Yes," Bernie answered, "I am a migrating bird and that is where we spend our winters, but my wings got stolen, that is why I'm riding a bike, but that is a long story."

"I wish I had the time to hear the story," the blue whale said, "but I am in a bit of a hurry to get up north. I am afraid to tell you that to get to the Indian Ocean you will need to pass through a storm, and this is the worst storm in years."

"I have heard about the storm," Bernie said, "but I met a dolphin and he said I would not need to pass through it."

"If you had not gone off course then it would not have been a problem," the blue whale said, "but to get to the Indian Ocean now, you will have no other choice than to go straight into the storm. I wished I could have helped you, but we are going in different directions. As soon we are through the seaweed, I can't give you a ride anymore."

"That's OK," said Bernie, "I understand."

The blue whale stopped when they had passed through all the seaweed of the Sargasso Sea.

Bernie had cleared out all the seaweed that had entangled in the bike's wheels, and once again he got back up in the saddle. He thanked the blue whale, who then continued on its journey up north. Bernie then started to pedal, once again on the right course to the Indian Ocean. But he had a knot in his stomach knowing he would soon have to encounter a terrifying storm.

As the evening started to approach, Bernie got closer to the storm, and he saw a big dark cloud in the horizon. Bernie took a deep breathe. The cloud was far too big to go around, so Bernie knew he would have to ride the bike straight into the storm. Bernie activated the breakwater function and the turbo engine. "This will be a wild ride," he said to himself.

That night was the worst night Bernie had experienced out on the ocean, actually, it was the worst night in Bernie's entire life. The rainfall was so heavy Bernie had trouble seeing anything, and he was so cold he was shaking. From time to time a huge wave would approach, but he had the breakwater function and the turbo engine to thank for not crashing into the waves. But, whenever Bernie started losing hope that the storm would never end, he thought about the warm tropical weather in the Indian Ocean and about seeing his family and friends again. He knew he could not give up and had to keep riding the bike. But what Bernie did not know is that while the heavy rain kept falling, and while he had to use all his focus to navigate around the big waves, he did not notice the signs that warned about entering into the shark passage and showed how to go around it. Bernie was now heading straight into the shark passage.

As dawn broke, the storm had finally started to subside, and the water was once again calm. Bernie could finally draw a big sigh of relief. He was completely exhausted from riding the bike through the storm, every muscle in his body was aching and he had not been able to get a single moment of sleep. *If I just close my eyes for a moment*, Bernie thought. It didn't take long until Bernie had fallen into a deep sleep, and he slowly drifted on the ocean and passed the last signs warning about entering the shark passage. Bernie was now in the shark passage.

A few hours later, Bernie woke up. *Oops*, he thought. I must have dozed off. But after checking his inner compass, he felt calm again; this time he had not gone off course. He was still heading straight to the Indian Ocean. Bernie had some breakfast, and then started to pedal again. After a while, he remembered about the dolphin he met. *The shark passage*, he thought to himself, *but I have not seen a single sign. Oh well, I guess I'll just be on the lookout for one.*

It had been a calm day out on the ocean when Bernie suddenly saw something jump out and in of the water. When Bernie came a little closer, he could see that it was a seal dressed in a party hat.

That is one lively seal, Bernie thought. The seal kept jumping in and out of the water and kept getting closer to Bernie who stopped the bike, thinking that the seal might want to say hello. When the seal got close Bernie thought it looked like the seal was trying to say something to him. He bent over a bit to hear what the seal was saying, but all he could hear was a word started with the letter S.

"S-s-shark," the seal who was out of breath managed to say.

Suddenly it dawned on Bernie what the seal was saying. Shark!

"Is the bicycle fast?" the seal wondered, gasping for air. "The shark is after me!"

"Jump in the basket," Bernie said, "this bicycle has a turbo engine."

The seal jumped into the basket and looked confused.

"A lot of fish you have here. Are you out on a fishing trip in the middle of the shark passage? You must be one strange bird."

Bernie tried to start the turbo engine, but nothing happened.

"Oh no," Bernie thought. The turbo engine had not recovered from the storm yet.

Bernie then started to pedal for all he was worth, but it was not too much use, as they both could see how the shark fin started to get closer to the bicycle with every second that passed.

"Did you not say you had a turbo engine?" the seal asked.

"I'm afraid it's not working at the moment," Bernie said.

"What will we do now?" the seal said desperately. "We will be shark food!"

At that moment they could hear a voice shouting,

"Come here! Come here!"

Bernie could see a very small ship with a human on it that frantically waved to them.

"Come here! Come here!" the human kept repeating.

"Well, go there!" the seal said.

"But it's a ship with a human," Bernie said, "that is dangerous."

"It is not a ship," the seal said, annoyed, "it's a sailboat. And it is either that or becoming shark food, I think it is an easy choice."

"I guess you are right," Bernie said, and started to pedal all he could in the direction of the sailboat.

"Faster!" the seal yelled. "The shark is catching up!"

Finally, they reached the sailboat, and the human pulled both of them up at the same moment the shark reached them. Both Bernie and the seal made it up to the boat at the last second, but the shark managed to grab a hold of the rear wheel of the bicycle. The shark soon released its grip when it realized it was not edible, and then the frustrated shark swam away. The human pulled the bicycle onto the boat.

"Unfortunately, the bicycle did not pull through as good as the both of you," the human said, and gave the bicycle back to Bernie.

A big piece of the rear wheel was missing, and you could clearly see the marks from the shark teeth. Bernie sat in a corner of the boat and exhaled.

"You don't need to be scared," the human said, "I will not harm you in any way."

"But you are a human," Bernie said, "I have heard one or two things about your kind, you put birds in cages and never let them see their friends and family again."

"And you make handbags out of seals," the seal said, upset. "At least that is what my aunt told me; would you like it if your family became handbags?"

"Of course not," the human said with a laugh, "but not all humans want to put birds in cages or make handbags out of seals. My name is Robert, and I am a lone sailor. I travel the oceans of the world by myself, and to do that you have to have respect for all the creatures of the sea. Including a seal in a party hat, or a bird riding a bike. Even though I have never encountered those before."

Bernie and the seal sat quiet for a while, looking around the sailboat.

"I don't see any cages or handbags," Bernie said.

"I don't either," said the seal, "and he did save us from becoming shark food."

"Okay," they both said at the same time, "we believe you."

"Good," Robert said. "Now may I ask what you both were doing in the middle of the shark passage on a bike?"

"I took a short cut," the seal said "I was in a rush to a birthday party, but that turned out to not be a very good idea.

I will definitely take the long way the next time. But I also wonder what the bird sitting next to me was doing out fishing in the shark passage?"

"I was not out on a fishing trip," Bernie answered. "I am a migrating bird; my name is Bernie. I let a rooster that I thought was my friend borrow my wings, but he stole my wings, so I borrowed a bike from a bear to get to the Indian Ocean. A dolphin had warned me about the shark passage, the dolphin said there were signs to show a way around it."

"There are signs," the seal said.

"Then I must have missed them," Bernie said, "I was riding the bike through a storm last night, I could hardly see my own beak."

"I have heard about you," Robert then said.

"What do you mean?" Bernie said, surprised.

"Two people took a picture of what looked like a bird riding a bicycle close to the Canary Islands."

"I remember those humans," Bernie said, "they had a weapon that was flashing when they were chasing me!"

"It was not a weapon," Robert explained, "they had a camera and they took pictures of you riding the bike, otherwise other people would not have believed them. But most people believe the picture was fake, so did I until I saw you myself."

"Most people?" Bernie said, confused. "Do many humans know about me?"

"Well, you are in the paper."

Robert took out a copy of a newspaper with a large image of Bernie riding the bike on the front page.

"Oh wow," Bernie said.

"This is really a very nice story," the seal said, bored, "but the fact is, I am wearing this ridiculous party hat for a reason. I am on my way to a birthday party. Would it be possible to ask for a ride out of the shark passage? I really don't feel like getting chased by another shark."

"Absolutely," Robert said, and took his position by the rudder. Where is the birthday party located?"

"I can just get off the boat when we've cleared the shark passage," said the seal. "No offense, but I would rather not show a human where we seals hang out."

"I understand," Robert said while the boat started to pick up some speed in the wind.

Bernie then looked at the destroyed rear wheel on the bike. How was he going to explain this to Bruno? And how would he be able to get to the Indian Ocean now?

Robert who noticed how devastated Bernie looked said calmly,

"I believe I can fix the bike for you, but it will probably take a while."

"Oh, thank you," Bernie said, relieved, "but where are you heading with the sail boat? Are you going in the same direction as the Indian Ocean?"

"I'm not really going in any specific direction," Robert said. "I usually just go wherever the wind takes me, but of course I can take a trip by the Indian Ocean and drop you off there."

"Oh, thank you!" Bernie said and got up from the corner of the boat to give Robert a hug.

"Be careful," the seal said, "remember that is a human."

"I know that," Bernie said, "but now I believe there are two kinds of humans, good and bad. And Robert is the good kind."

A few hours later, the sailboat had passed through the shark passage, and Bernie and Robert waved goodbye to the seal that rushed away to get to the birthday party.

"Alright," Robert said, "we have a good and stable wind at the moment. I guess I can sit down for a while now and take a look at the bicycle."

Robert took out a toolbox, and looked a little troubled as he checked the bicycle.

"This rear wheel will not be easy to fix, but it's not impossible."

"Do you fix bicycles often?" Bernie asked.

"I actually used to be a professional cyclist," Robert said, "but after a few years I realized it was sailing that was my big passion in life. So, I sold my bicycles and bought a sailboat, and from that day on I have been sailing around the world."

"But don't you get lonely?" Bernie asked. "Sometimes I feel terribly lonely on my bike ride."

"It is a part of the experience," Robert explained, "to be together with friends and family is fun, but when you are on your own, facing challenges, that is when you really get to know who you are. Tell me, Bernie, have you not learned a lot on your bike ride?"

Bernie thought about his adventures on the oceans. He had saved a dolphin baby, ridden a whale, bicycled through a storm, and met Can-Can. The most beautiful bird he had ever seen.

"Yes," Bernie answered. "Before I left Featherbay, I never thought I could make it to the Indian Ocean without my wings. Now it feels like I can do anything."

"Featherbay?" Robert said. "Is that where you are from?"

"Yes," Bernie said, "but that is a secret. Only birds are allowed to know where Featherbay is."

"You birds and seals are secretive creatures," Robert said laughing. "So only birds live in Featherbay?"

"Well, only birds and one bear," Bernie said, "it was the bear's bike I was allowed to borrow."

"A bear," Robert said, impressed. "Well, it certainly is a fine bike, we are just lucky humans can help fix them."

Bernie felt that it was nice to take a break from riding the bike for a while. He could now peacefully look at the ocean from the sailboat that would bring him to the Indian Ocean.

We are on the right path, Bernie thought. *I can feel that inside me.*

After two calm days out on the ocean, Bernie woke up at dawn by Robert shouting in excitement,

"Bernie, wake up! You have to see this!"

Drowsy Bernie got up and looked out at the ocean in the direction Robert was pointing. Bernie could see a sign, he focused to be able to see what the sign said.

"I-I-Indian Ocean! It says Indian Ocean!" Bernie said, and almost couldn't believe it.

"Yes, it does," Robert said. "It's not far to go now."

Bernie was now wide awake, and jumped around in the sailboat. He was so excited he could not sit still for a second.

"I have fixed the bike now," Robert said. "The bear you

borrowed it from should not be able to notice the shark attack."

"Thank you," Bernie said, and took a look at the bike.

The bike looked as perfect as the day he had left Featherbay.

"But before it's time for you to leave, I must take a picture of you and the bike," Robert said.

"A picture," Bernie responded, "is that one of those things that ended up in the paper?"

"Not this picture," Robert said, "but then at least I will be able to show the people I meet at the next port that I met the cycling migrating bird, Bernie."

"Ok then," Bernie said. He put on his helmet, jumped up at the saddle and smiled.

"That's lovely," Robert said, and took out his camera. "This time you don't have to be scared of the flash."

Robert took the picture and put the camera back before saying to Bernie,

"If you look out to the west now, I think you will see a long-awaited sight."

Bernie looked to the west, and, besides Can-Can's big eyes, what he now saw was the most beautiful thing he had ever looked at. On the horizon, he saw an island resting in turquoise water. The beach had white sand, and palm trees slowly rocked in the warm breeze.

"You did it Bernie," Robert said, "you made it to the Indian Ocean without your wings."

"Yes," Bernie said, "I really did it."

"I think it's for the best if you ride the bike the final part to the island, so your friends and family don't see that you've been on a sail boat with a human."

"It's ok," Bernie said, "I will tell them that there is such a thing as a good human, but I would like to ride the bike to the island."

"Just give me the bike for a second," Robert said.

"Is there something wrong with it?" Bernie asked, worried.

"Oh no," Robert said, and took out a screwdriver.

After a little while Robert handed Bernie back the bike, but it didn't quite look the same. Robert had taken off the training wheels.

"But," Bernie said, perplexed, "how am I going to be able to ride the bike now?"

"I think you are ready to ride the bike without training wheels now," Robert said calmly.

"But," Bernie continued.

"We will never know unless you try," Robert said. "Get up on the bike now."

Hesitant, Bernie got back up on the bike in the turquoise water and attempted to ride the bike. He was worried he was going to lose his balance, but to his great surprise it went fine.

"Look, Robert!" Bernie shouted happily. "I am riding the bike without training wheels!"

"I knew you could," Robert said proudly, and put the training wheels in the basket on the bike.

"I remember what you said, the bicycle is a loan, and needs to be returned in the same condition as it was when you borrowed it."

"Thank you for everything Robert," Bernie said, "I will never forget you."

"I will never forget you either," Robert said, "but who knows, maybe we will meet out on the ocean again."

"I hope so," Bernie said while a tear ran down his feathers.

"Don't cry," Robert said, "there will always be a place for you in my sailboat and in my heart."

With these words, Robert sailed away, looking for more adventures out on the ocean. Now all Bernie had left was a very short bike ride until he would be reunited with his friends and family. The turquoise water was so clear he could see the multi colored fish his parents told him he would find in these tropical waters. Bernie had now reached the beach, and he put his feet down in the warm sand and pulled the bike up on the beach with his beak. The beach looked deserted, and the only sound he could hear was the sound the palm trees made from the warm breeze and the small waves hitting the beach.

Bernie started to think about how he would find his family and friends. *Maybe I start making my way more inwards of the island*, Bernie thought. *It is probably there they have built the bird's nest for the winter*. At the same moment, he thought he heard a familiar voice,

"Bernie! Bernie is here!"

Wingy came running down the beach, closely followed by Beaky. The three friends embraced in a hug.

"You did it!" Wingy shouted. "You cycled to the Indian Ocean!"

Then Bernie could see his parents running towards him.

"My son!" Bernie's mother shouted while embracing Bernie together with his father.

"You really have shown what being a migrating bird is

all about," Bernie's father said proudly. "A true migrating bird doesn't need wings, only courage and determination."

All the migrating birds from Featherbay had now gathered on the beach to wish Bernie welcome.

"We will have a big party tonight to celebrate your arrival," Bernie's mother said.

Wingy then grabbed Bernie and pulled him away from the crowd.

"Bernie, there's something you need to know."

"What is it?" Bernie said, a bit concerned about the serious tone in Wingy's voice.

"Rooster Bob is here," Wingy said.

"Bob!" Bernie said, shocked. "Where is he?"

"Over there," Wingy said, pointing with his wing.

Then Bernie could see Bob sitting at the root of a palm tree further down the beach. His head was hanging, and his shoulders tilted forward, and he seemed completely unaware of the joyous celebration taking place on the beach. Then Bernie could see that it was not only Bob that had made it to the Indian Ocean; so had his wings.

"My wings," Bernie said quietly, "my wings are here.

"Yes," Wingy said. "Bob has your wings, and they seem totally unharmed. Bob was already sitting underneath that palm tree when we got to the Indian Ocean a few days ago. He has not said a word to anyone, he just sits there by himself."

"Well, maybe Bob will talk to me," Bernie said. "I definitely want to talk to him."

Bernie started walking towards the palm tree Bob was sitting under, but Bob did not notice Bernie approaching him.

"Hey Bob," Bernie said when he stopped right next to the sitting rooster.

Bob finally looked up, and his facial expression turned from miserable to joyous when he saw Bernie.

"Bernie!" Bob shouted and flew up. "You are here, I thought I had ruined everything for you!"

Bob then looked very confused before asking,

"But how did you get here?"

"I bicycled," Bernie said.

Bob still looked very confused.

"But why did you steal my wings, Bob?" Bernie asked, disappointed. "It was a loan, you promised me you would give them back to me right away, not fly with them to the Indian Ocean!"

"Oh, Bernie," Bob said, and dramatically sat down again in the sand. "I was going to give you your wings back, I really was. I felt so proud when I was flying to the hen house to show Franny that I could fly, but when I got there Franny still said she wouldn't marry me. I was so devastated I thought I might just keep flying. If Franny didn't want to marry I didn't want to stay in Featherbay. Eventually I ended up here, it was like your wings knew the way to the Indian Ocean, but I felt so bad since I landed here having stolen your wings.

Bernie sat down next to Bob in the sand.

"Bob, you have misunderstood the whole thing. Franny told you that she wanted a rooster, not a migrating bird. All she wants is you being who you are, a rooster. Well yes, your 'cock-a-doodle-do' is very off pitch, but you can find professional help for that in Featherbay. Franny wants to marry you!"

"What?" Bob said, surprised. "Did she tell you that?"

"Yes," Bernie answered, "she told me right before I went on my bike ride."

"Oh dear," Bob said, and once again flew up from underneath the palm tree. "What am I doing in the Indian Ocean if I have a fiancé in Featherbay?"

"I wonder that too," Bernie said with a laugh.

"Oh well," Bob said, and once again sat down. "The most important thing now is that I return your wings to you. I will hitchhike or something like that back to Featherbay."

Bob leaned forward to remove the wings, but Bernie stopped him.

"No," Bernie said, "take my wings and fly back to Featherbay. You can keep them safe until I return."

"Are you sure?" Bob said, surprised.

"Yes," Bernie answered, "you need my wings more than I do at the moment. And the bicycle I got here on is borrowed. I need to make sure it gets back to Featherbay."

"Oh Bernie," Bob said, and gave him a hug. "You really are a good friend."

"It's alright," Bernie said, "now come on, time for you to fly back to your fiancé."

Bob got ready, and after flapping the wings a few times he took off to fly back to Featherbay.

Wingy, who saw Bob fly away, ran up to Bernie.

"Bernie! Bob is flying away with your wings, and you just sit here, I will fly after the crazy rooster!"

"No need to," Bernie said, "I gave Bob an extended loan period for my wings, and I would rather ride the bicycle home in the spring."

"Did you lose your mind out on the ocean?" Wingy said, shocked.

"No, not at all," Bernie said, standing up. "I enjoy riding the bicycle. Bob may have stolen my wings, but that gave me an adventure I will remember forever. I also have someone to meet on the way home, and she expects me to get there on the water, not in the air."

"Oh, a 'she'?" Wingy said curiously. "You must tell me everything at the party tonight! Now let's go, I'm getting hungry."

"Well, that was a surprise," Bernie laughed.

Wingy put his wing around his friend, and they slowly went back to the rest of the migrating birds on the beach. The sun started to descend after another day shining on them. Finally, everybody had arrived, and they could start preparing for the big party tonight, and a winter together in paradise.

About the Author

My name is Victoria Fredriksson and my biggest passion is writing and making stories come alive.

Acknowledgements

Thank you to my father, Kjell, for always being there for me.

Lightning Source UK Ltd.
Milton Keynes UK
UKHW042332230522
403422UK00004B/81